Twilight Sparkle's Spell

HASBRO and its logo, MY LITTLE PONY and all related characters are trademarks of Hasbro and are used with permission. © 2017 HASBRO. All Rights Reserved.

Cover design by Véronique Lefèvre Sweet and Christina Quintero.

Little, Brown and Company
Hachette Book Group
1290 Avenue of the Americas, New York, NY 10104
Visit us at LBYR.com
mylittlepony.com

First published as *Twilight Sparkle and the Crystal Heart Spell*
by Little, Brown and Company in April 2013;
Originally adapted in 2017 by Five Mile, an imprint of
Bonnier Publishing Australia in Australia.
First U.S. Edition: March 2019

Little, Brown and Company is a division of Hachette Book Group, Inc.
The Little, Brown name and logo are trademarks of Hachette Book Group, Inc.

The publisher is not responsible for websites (or their content)
that are not owned by the publisher.

Library of Congress Control Number 2018946078

ISBNs: 978-0-316-48810-5 (pbk.), 978-0-316-48811-2 (ebook)

Printed in the United States of America

LSC-C

Licensed By:

Twilight Sparkle's Spell

G. M. Berrow

LITTLE, BROWN AND COMPANY

NEW YORK ✳ BOSTON

Chapter 1

Twilight Sparkle has just been crowned a princess of Equestria. When she was crowned, Princess Celestia gave Twilight her own set of wings. *Real* Pegasus wings! Now Twilight Sparkle is an Alicorn.

Twilight Sparkle's magical powers and bravery have made her famous across Equestria. Everypony is excited about the great things Twilight will do as a princess. Twilight is proud to be a princess, but nervous, too. Could she really lead a whole pony kingdom one day?

* * *

Since being crowned, Twilight has spent a lot of time at her favorite place:

the Golden Oak Library. She is looking for books about how to be a great leader. Spike, her Dragon friend, is helping, too. One day, Spike looks up from a book called *Daring Do and the Terrifying Tower*. "That's it!" he cries.

Twilight frowns. She has already read this book. "What does *Daring Do* have to do with it?"

"Daring Do asks a wise pony how to overcome her fears...."

Twilight's face lights up. Of course! She needs guidance from a wise pony. "Good work, Spike!"

Spike blushes. But before he can speak, Twilight Sparkle is gone.

Chapter 2

Twilight trots into the town square.

"Who in Ponyville can teach me about being a leader?" she wonders. She sees Mayor Mare trotting to the town hall. Perfect! But when Twilight gets to the town hall, the mayor is gone.

"Sorry, Princess Twilight Sparkle," says the guard pony. "Ms. Mayor Mare has an important meeting."

"That's okay," Twilight says. "And, you don't have to call me, um, *Princess*. Just *Twilight* will do." Twilight is a little embarrassed by such an important-sounding title.

"Yes, Princess Twilight. I mean, *Just Twilight!*" says the guard.

Twilight smiles reassuringly and trots off.

"Fresh cupcakes!" shouts Carrot Cake, the town baker, pulling his cart into the square. Twilight's tummy rumbles as she joins a line of hungry ponies.

"Hello, Mr. Cake!" Twilight says when it is her turn. "One cupcake please."

"Oh dear. None left!" Mr. Cake says. "Come back to Sugarcube Corner with me. Mrs. Cake will have more."

Twilight should be getting advice, not eating cupcakes! But her tummy rumbles again, so she follows Mr. Cake.

$*$ $*$ $*$

"Mrs. Cake, this rainbow-chip delight is ... *mmmf* ... delicious," Twilight mumbles around her mouthful. "I'm sorry to eat and fly, but I really must be off."

"Of course, Princess," Mrs. Cake says, bowing quickly.

"Please. Don't call me that. I'm still just the same old Twilight," Twilight says, blushing. Suddenly all her worries spill out. "I mean, I don't even know how to be a princess. I'm trying to ask some older ponies how to be a leader. But Mayor Mare was busy, and..."

"My goodness," says Mrs. Cake. "How tricky. Why don't you ask your brother and Princess Cadance?"

Twilight brightens. Shining Armor and her Pegasister-in-law, Princess Cadance, have lots of royal experience.

"You're a genius, Mrs. Cake! Thank you!" says Twilight. She flies to the Crystal Empire that very day.

Chapter 3

The Crystal Empire is even more
beautiful than the last time Twilight
Sparkle was there. The winding cobble-
gem streets and tall glass spires sparkle
in the sunshine. Crystal ponies smile as

they trot past. Some call, "Hey, Princess Twilight Sparkle!" or "Welcome back!"

"Good afternoon, everypony," Twilight replies, smiling and waving.

The Crystal Empire kingdom is bursting with happiness and love. What a perfect place for Shining Armor and Princess Cadance to live and rule!

"Twily!" shouts Shining Armor, running over. "How's my second-favorite princess?"

"Hey!" Twilight laughs.

"Only kidding!" he says. "You're
both my favorites."

Princess Cadance trots over to
join them.

"Cadance!" Twilight calls out happily.

"Sunshine…sunshine…" she starts.

"Ladybugs awake!" Cadance yells.

"Clap your hooves and do a little shake!" The two princesses sing together as they hop around and shake their tails. This has been their secret tailshake since Twilight was a little filly and Cadance was her foal-sitter. It is still really fun to do!

"So what brings you to the Crystal

Empire, sis?" Shining Armor asks. "Isn't royal life great?"

"Well, that's why I'm here." Twilight drops her eyes to the ground. "I don't know how to be a leader. And I don't feel like a princess. I don't know what to do."

"Oh, Twilight!" says Shining Armor. "You're doing great!"

"Of course you would say that. You're my brother," says Twilight.

"Relax, Twily. Being royalty is easy! Right, Cadance?" Shining Armor replies. But Cadance's face is serious.

"No, Shining. It's not as simple as that." Cadance turns to Twilight. "Maybe I can help you."

Chapter 4

"You're such a great princess, Cadance," Twilight says as the two ponies walk through the Crystal Empire. "I wish I could be like you. I feel so lost."

"You know, I didn't always feel so confident," Cadance admits.

"You didn't?" Twilight asks.

"I'd always been told what a great leader I would be, but I didn't know what to do!" Cadance says. Twilight nods. That's just how she feels.

"So," Cadance says, "I went to Princess Celestia for advice."

"And?" Twilight asks, all ears.

"She asked me if I felt like a true leader," says Cadance. "I didn't. Then

Princess Celestia told me about an ancient spell. The spell turns any future leader into the pony they are meant to be."

Twilight brightens. Magic—of course!

They stop at the famous Crystal Heart, which is powered by the magic of the Crystal ponies.

"So, where can I find this leadership spell?" asks Twilight. "Can you teach me?"

"Oh no, Twilight," says Cadance. "The spell isn't something you can teach. The Crystal Heart Spell will be revealed when you understand what your biggest leadership challenge will be. Only then will you know, in your heart, how to rule."

Twilight frowns. "How in the hoof am I supposed to know that?"

"The spell works differently for everypony. I can help you with just one clue," Cadance says. "The same clue

Princess Celestia gave me when I first became a princess: Think about what makes a great kingdom."

"The Elements of Harmony?" asks Twilight.

"Not quite," says Cadance. She explains how she went about finding the answer: "I started by asking my friends what they thought would make a great kingdom. They had all sorts of crazy ideas, and I listened to each one. But I still couldn't figure out what the spell was.

"One day, I was sitting by the lake, thinking," recalls Cadance. "I realized I listened only to other ponies. I never made my own decisions. As soon as I realized this, shimmering gold letters appeared on the lake. It was the spell!"

"Wow," says Twilight.

"The spell showed me I would lead other ponies with True Love and Tolerance," Cadance continues. "But the only way I could do it was by listening to my *own* heart, too."

Chapter 5

That night, Cadance leads Twilight into a lush castle bedroom. Twilight blinks in disbelief. "This room is all mine?"

"Well, not all yours!" says Spike,

popping out from behind the purple
curtains.

"Spike!" Twilight exclaims, instantly
feeling guilty. "Sorry I left Ponyville in

such a rush. You know how I get when I'm on a mission."

"Do I ever!" says Spike.

Cadance gives Twilight a small box with a bow on top. "Just a little gift from one princess to another," she says with a wink.

Inside is a beautiful necklace made of purple jewels. At the center is a large heart-shaped gem. Twilight recognizes it at once. "Cadance, this is your favorite necklace!"

Cadance smiles warmly. "I think it's time for a new princess to wear it."

"Oh, Cadance! Thank you."

"Of course," Cadance says. "There's just one thing."

"Yes?" says Twilight distractedly as she puts on the necklace.

"The gem in the middle is made of Cosmic Spectrum," Cadance explains. "As long as you are filled with the magic of love and positivity, the necklace will wrap you in warmth and protection."

"Whoa!" Twilight says, looking down at the rare gem.

"But remember," warns Cadance, "if you think negative or bad thoughts, the necklace will make you feel worse! Stay true to your heart and the spell will reveal itself."

Twilight Sparkle nods. She will not forget.

The next morning, Twilight wants to

start looking for the spell straightaway. But where should she start?

Twilight puts on the necklace. She immediately knows just what to do. "Cadance asked her friends for their ideas. I'll do that, too!"

Chapter 6

Twilight Sparkle goes back home to Ponyville. She already sent Spike ahead to ask her friends to a secret meeting at the Golden Oak Library. That night, her friends arrive at the library. Little do they know that nosy Gilda the Griffon has heard about the meeting and is eavesdropping from outside the cottage!

＊　　＊　　＊

"So what is this secret meeting all about, Twilight?" Applejack asks.

Twilight smiles at her friends, all there to help her. The thought fills her with warmth, making her necklace shine.

"Thank you all for coming—" she begins, but Rarity interrupts.

"*Ohh*, is that necklace made of Cosmic Spectrum? It's gorgeous!" Rarity leans in for a closer look.

"Thanks! It was a present from Princess Cadance."

"You know what they say about Cosmic Spectrum," Rarity adds. "When you wear it, you must remember—"

"Oh yeah, Cadance told me all about

it." Twilight cuts her off. She wants to get the meeting going.

Rarity sits back, a little hurt.

"Anyway, thank you all for coming on such short notice," Twilight continues. "I've asked you here because I need your help."

Twilight tells the ponies about the Crystal Heart Spell. She explains that she can find it only with the help of her friends.

"I need you to help me figure out what makes a great kingdom. Otherwise I'll never find the spell, and then I'll never learn how to lead!" Twilight says dramatically.

"Don't worry, Twilight," Fluttershy says. "We'll figure this out."

"So you'll help me?" Twilight asks hopefully.

The ponies nod. "Together!"

Chapter 7

The ponies chat for hours, but Twilight isn't sure it's helping. They all have very different ideas about what makes a great kingdom.

Pinkie Pie suggests an official Cake

Day. Rainbow Dash wants a Royal Guard of the fastest ponies in the kingdom. Applejack wants ponies to always have dinner with their families. Fluttershy suggests a nature reserve for baby animals. Twilight sighs. She needs real ideas, not silly ones. "Rarity, any ideas? You're awfully quiet."

"Well, sure ... if you *actually* want *my* opinion," Rarity grumbles. Since trying to warn Twilight about the necklace, Rarity hasn't said a word. "I would

design a fashion line for the kingdom
so everypony could look and feel their
best."

Twilight rolls her eyes. "Fashion,
Rarity?"

"Sorry if my idea isn't good enough,
Princess," Rarity snaps, trotting out in a
huff.

Twilight finally realizes she has hurt Rarity's feelings. "I'm sorry, Rarity. I didn't mean to upset you. Thanks, everypony. I guess that's enough for tonight."

Chapter 8

Gilda the Griffon waits until the last pony has left. As Twilight waves her friends off, Gilda swoops down.

"Finally!" she says, landing in front

of Twilight. "I thought they would never leave. Good meeting?"

"Hey! How did you know about the meeting?" Twilight asks.

"I have my ways," Gilda says. "I heard the whole thing. Didn't sound like your friends had any good ideas...."

"So what would you do, Gilda?" asks Twilight.

"If I were a princess, I wouldn't listen to anyone else. I would do whatever I wanted!" Gilda cackles and flies off.

Twilight frowns and goes back inside. Gilda is a mischief maker. Everypony knows that. But Twilight has to admit, her friends don't seem to know much about being royal.

Maybe Gilda has a point. Maybe the

secret to leadership is listening to your own heart, instead of everypony else's.

If I'm going to be a real princess, maybe I need to start acting like one, Twilight thinks.

*   *   *

Trying to find the Crystal Heart Spell is starting to drive Twilight crazy. Nothing she tries seems to work, and nopony has any good ideas. It's so odd—ever since Gilda suggested that Twilight shouldn't listen to her friends, Twilight has felt that everypony else's opinions are wrong. Twilight takes a trot in the forest to think things through. But soon the noise of crashing leaves breaks into Twilight's thoughts.

"There you are!" Pinkie Pie shouts.

"Come see my plans for the holiday celebrations!"

"Now isn't a good time, Pinkie," Twilight says. "I'm sort of busy."

"Oh. Will you be busy in ten minutes?" Pinkie asks.

"Yes." Twilight wants to be alone.

"What about in twenty minutes?" Pinkie asks.

"Yes, Pinkie! I'm busy!" Twilight snaps. Her necklace begins to dim, and the colors churn. "I don't have time to talk about silly parties."

"Oh," says Pinkie quietly. "Sorry, Twilight. I was just trying to help."

Pinkie trots off sadly, wondering what's going on with Twilight Sparkle.

Chapter 9

Twilight Sparkle is looking for Gilda the Griffon. There has to be more to what she tried to tell Twilight the other night after the meeting. Twilight finds Gilda at Sweet Apple Acres with Trixie. They are filling an empty cider barrel with some gloopy green gunk as part of a mean prank.

"Hey!" shouts Twilight. "You two! Come here!"

"Are you finally giving orders of your own, like a *real* princess?" Gilda sneers. "Or are you just here to tattle on us to Applejack?"

"I couldn't care less what you do with that cider," Twilight snaps, promising herself she'll warn Granny Smith later about the slime. "I'm here because ... I want to ask you about ..." Twilight can't quite find the words to ask Gilda for help.

Trixie is wearing her purple magician's robe and pointy hat. "The Great and Powerful Trixie doesn't have all day!" she says, tapping her hoof.

"Gilda, what were you talking about the other night?" Twilight asks.

The Griffon shrugs. "I was just saying

that if I were a princess, I wouldn't let anypony tell me what to do. I would trust my own ideas." Gilda puts her claw on Twilight's shoulder. "What is it that *you* want to do, Twilight?"

Twilight hesitates. *Gilda has a point*, thinks Twilight. *Why am I asking my friends when I know exactly where to find*

the answers? The one place I always feel

completely at ease.

"I want to go to the library! The Crystal Empire Library!" she says.

Gilda nods slowly. "The library thing is a little weird. But the Crystal Empire sounds awesome! Right on, Princess Twilight!"

Twilight's necklace begins to darken even more. But she doesn't notice.

Chapter 10

All Twilight can think about is the huge library in the Crystal Empire. It holds hundreds of old books—the spell must be in one of them! She can't wait to get started.

"Thanks for your help, guys," Twilight tells Gilda and Trixie. "I'm going right now!"

Twilight spreads her wings and takes off.

"I'm coming, too," Gilda says, flying alongside her. "What are the ponies like in the Crystal Empire?" Gilda imagines all the ponies she can play pranks on. She thinks it will be so funny!

"Trixie will come, too!" Trixie exclaims, trotting beneath them. She pictures a whole city of ponies who haven't seen her magic act yet!

On the ground below, Fluttershy is leading a line of baby ducklings back to their mother. Suddenly she notices Twilight in the sky. "Oh, hi, Twilight!" she says. "I'm so glad you're here! I've come up with some new ideas—"

But Twilight swooshes past. She doesn't even see Fluttershy.

Rarity is nearby and watches in pure shock. The Twilight who Rarity knows would always stop to talk with her friends.

As Twilight passes, Rarity notices that the magical gem on her necklace has lost some of its shine. This is a bad sign.

"Oh, Fluttershy!" Rarity says, trotting up to her friend.

"She must not have heard me,"

Fluttershy says quietly. "Twilight would never ignore me on purpose, right?"

Before Rarity can mention the necklace, Gilda lets Twilight fly out of earshot and then calls down to them. "Twilight is a princess now! She doesn't need silly friends like you holding her back."

Rarity and Fluttershy exchange a worried look. "We'd better go find Spike," says Rarity. "He'll know what to do."

Chapter 11

Rarity and Fluttershy knock on the door of the Golden Oak Library.

The door flings open. Spike is upset.

"Are you okay, Spike?" Fluttershy asks softly.

"Twilight left me behind again!" Spike wails.

"*Hmm*...Twilight is not acting like herself today," Rarity says. "I think her necklace is to blame!"

"Huh?" Spike and Fluttershy say.

"That necklace can be dangerous. If the wearer has bad or sad feelings, the gem makes them feel worse! I tried to warn Twilight the other night, but she just wouldn't listen."

"Oh no!" says Fluttershy.

"Poor Twilight." Spike jumps up. "We have to go save her. Together?"

"Together!" shout Fluttershy and Rarity. The friends find Applejack, Pinkie Pie, and Rainbow Dash, and they all go to find Twilight.

As Twilight Sparkle reaches the Crystal Empire, she turns to Gilda and Trixie. "Go and do what you want," she snaps. "Just stay out of my way!"

Twilight gallops to the library, and she runs into Shining Armor.

"Twily!" Shining Armor says. "I thought you went back to Ponyville."

"I did, but I'm back again," Twilight says, itching to get to the library.

"Great!" Shining Armor says. "Come and have lunch at the castle."

"Er, maybe tomorrow," Twilight says, and then she canters off.

Shining Armor watches her go. *There is something wrong with Twilight*, he thinks. He rushes off to find Princess Cadance to help.

∗ ∗ ∗

In the library, Twilight Sparkle flips the pages of *Ancient Spells of the Crystal Empire: Volume Four*. She has already checked the first three volumes. The Crystal Heart Spell must be in here somewhere!

"Twilight! Are you in here?" Princess Cadance's voice echoes through the library.

"I'm here." Twilight sighs. She doesn't want to tell Cadance she hasn't found the spell yet.

"Oh dear," Cadance says, seeing Twilight. "It's just as I feared."

"What?" Twilight whines. "Me being a big failure? A pony with no leadership skills? I should give back my crown."

"You're not a failure," Cadance says. She points at Twilight's necklace. The gem isn't shining at all now. "Look!

You're so down on yourself, the necklace is making you feel worse!"

Twilight looks at the gem. "I didn't even notice it had changed."

Twilight suddenly thinks of her friends. Rarity tried to warn her about the gemstone, but Twilight didn't listen.

Actually, Twilight had dismissed all their ideas. They had only been trying to help her, just as she'd asked them to.

And how had she thanked them? By ignoring them.

"Oh, Cadance, I've been so mean to my friends!" Twilight says. "I've been thinking only about what I want, and not listening to other ponies!" The gem around her neck begins to glow dimly. "I must find my friends and apologize—right now!"

Chapter 12

"I wonder where Twilight is," says Applejack as she and her friends enter the Crystal Empire.

"What's that?!" says Pinkie Pie, pointing to a large crowd.

"Let's find out!" says Applejack.

They see a big striped tent. Posters hang on the sides, advertising THE GREAT AND POWERFUL TRIXIE.

Gilda the Griffon is standing on an old apple crate.

"Step right up, Crystal ponies!" she shouts. "See Equestria's most talented Unicorn, the Great and Powerful Trixie! Only three bits each!"

A yellow pony pays Gilda and enters the tent.

"Don't they know it's a scam?" asks Rainbow Dash.

Gilda, unaware of the Ponyville crew, continues, "Trixie is so powerful, she once defeated an ursa major!"

"Hey, it was Twilight who did that!" says Fluttershy. "Except it was an ursa minor."

"I can't watch this," Applejack says, hopping onto another crate. "Crystal ponies! Do not pay to see this show! This Griffon and Unicorn are trying to steal your bits!" A low murmur buzzes through the crowd.

"What are you doing here?!" Gilda screeches.

The Crystal ponies look on in alarm. This argument is more of a show than they'd expected!

"Nopony wants you here!" Gilda yells. But she couldn't have been more wrong.

"That's not true!" A clear, strong voice pierces through the crowd.

It's Twilight Sparkle!

"These are my best friends, and I want them here!" She trots over. "What are you guys doing here?"

"We came to rescue you, silly!" says Pinkie Pie.

"I told them about the necklace," Rarity explains. "We knew you weren't yourself."

"The Twilight we know would never be mean to her friends!" Fluttershy adds.

"Or ditch us for those two!" Rainbow Dash finishes, motioning to Gilda and Trixie.

"I'm so sorry, you guys!" Twilight says. "I thought listening to my heart meant choosing what I wanted for the kingdom. But what matters is how a princess treats others, especially her friends." She pulls them all into a group hug. "Princess or not—we are all equal ponies!"

Rarity squeals. "Twilight, look at

your necklace!"

The gem glows brighter than ever

before. The light pulsates, like a true beating heart.

Nearby, the Crystal Heart grows brighter, too. It's almost as if the two jewels are linked somehow. Suddenly a gigantic rainbow bursts from the Crystal Heart and arches into Twilight's necklace!

"Ooooooh!" coos the crowd.

"Hey, look!" Rainbow Dash shouts.

"There are words on the Crystal Heart!" Twilight gasps. It must be the

Crystal Heart Spell! She takes a deep breath and reads the words aloud:

"Friendship is the creed.
It has been from the start.
It's the only way to lead
with your Crystal Heart!"

Of course! Friendship has always been the answer to her problems. Why should it be any different now that she's a princess?

Twilight glances at her best friends, her brother, and Cadance, looking proud. She hears the crowd of Crystal ponies cheering her on.

At last, Twilight feels like a real princess.